Duggy Dog looked out of the window.

Snow was falling, and the garden wasn't green any more.

Mrs Smith opened the kitchen door. She threw some bread out for the birds, so Duggy Dog went outside.

A robin flew down to peck at a crust.

"What's this all over the garden?"
Duggy Dog asked the robin.

"Snow," said the robin.

"I've seen it before, but not for a long
time," said Duggy Dog.

"It comes in the winter time," explained
the robin.

Duggy Dog rolled in the snow until he
was white all over. Then he shook himself
and told the robin he was going to see if his
friends liked the snow too.

Off he ran, across the garden, over the fence, and over the Big Field to call for little Jasper.

"What's that outside, Duggy Dog?" said Jasper through the flap of his little dog-door.

"Snow," said Duggy Dog.

Jasper said he didn't think he liked it.

"You will," said Duggy Dog. "Come on!"

Off they ran out onto the Big Field.

Jasper shivered at first but soon began to enjoy the snow.

"Now what do we do?" said Jasper.

"Dig holes," said Duggy Dog.

Up flew the snow, *swissh-swissh*!

"Isn't it great, Jasper!" called Duggy
Dog, but Jasper didn't answer him.

He looked all around, but he couldn't see
his friend.

"Where's my friend Jasper?" Duggy Dog
called to the robin who had been eating
crusts in his garden.

"Here," said the robin, and she hopped
over the snow.

Duggy Dog looked.

And there was Jasper, in a deep
snowdrift.

It was so deep that he couldn't get out of
it!

Duggy Dog jumped down into the hole
and Jasper scrambled out over him.

"You're right, Duggy Dog!" said Jasper.
"Snow is great. Let's go and tell Floss and
Minty!"

They went, jumping in and out of the
snowdrifts across the Big Field.

Floss was glad to see them.

"Come and roll in the snow!" called Duggy Dog.

"You can dig holes in it. But not too deep," Jasper told her.

So that's what they did.

They rolled in the snow and shook it all off again. They dug more holes, then Duggy Dog said it was time to call for Minty.

"Minty won't come out to play," said Floss.

"Why not?" said Duggy Dog.

"Because of the monster," said Floss.

"A monster!" cried Jasper.

He looked all around. So did Duggy Dog. They couldn't see anything that looked like a monster.

"Where is it, Floss?" said Duggy Dog.

"I didn't see it when I called for Minty this morning, but she said it's hiding in the corner of the Big Field," said Floss.

"Well, what sort of monster is it?" asked little Jasper.

"Horrible!" Floss told her friends. "And Minty said it's got a big brown hat on its head, too!"

Jasper didn't like the sound of the monster outside Minty's garden. He said he was scared, and he would like to go home if Duggy Dog would go with him, please.

But Floss said they should try and help
Minty.

"You're not afraid of the monster, are
you, Duggy Dog?" she asked him.

"Umm, er, no, course not!" he said.

They all set off for Minty's house.

She was hiding behind the shed in her
garden.

"Come out and play in the Big Field!"
called Duggy Dog.

"No! There's a horrible monster out
there!" she cried.

Duggy Dog looked all around. He
couldn't see anything that looked like a
monster. Then the robin who had been
pecking at the crust came hopping along.

"Where's Minty's monster?" said Duggy
Dog to the robin.

"I don't know," she told him. "I'm
hungry. I wish I could find some nuts for a
change. 'Bye, Duggy Dog!"

Duggy Dog told Minty he couldn't see a
monster outside her garden.

"Are you sure?" asked Minty.

"Of course," said Duggy Dog. "Come
on, Minty!"

Minty decided she would be brave, like her friends. She jumped over the fence and followed Duggy Dog past a big snowdrift.

And there was the monster!

"There it is!" she cried.

"The monster!" cried Jasper.

"The one with the big brown hat!" cried Floss.

It was just as Floss had told them.

It was huge and white and horrible! And it had blue buttons for eyes, a red carrot for a nose, and a big brown hat on its head. The four dogs all backed away.

Then the robin hopped along and flew up onto the monster's big brown hat.

Duggy Dog watched the monster for a few moments.

It didn't seem to be looking at him, so he went a little closer to it.

"Aren't you scared of Minty's monster?" Duggy Dog asked the robin.

"No," she said. "It's not a monster, it's a snowman."

"It wasn't there yesterday," Minty said.

"There wasn't any snow yesterday, that's why," the robin told her. "The children made it before they went to school this morning."

Then the robin pecked at the snowman's carrot nose.

Minty was still a bit scared, so Duggy Dog ran to fetch her.

"Watch out, Duggy Dog!" cheeped the robin. "The children made a slippery slide as well!"

Duggy Dog didn't hear the robin.

Off he ran.

He ran straight onto the slide. It felt very odd. His legs didn't seem to want to run, but he was still going very fast.

"Look out, you're going straight towards the monster!" Minty cried, but Duggy Dog went faster and faster down the slide.

Slosssh-sprossshh! he crashed into the snowman!

Up flew the robin.

"I told you, Duggy Dog!" she cheeped.

Duggy Dog sat up and looked around.
The snowman had gone.

All that was left was a heap of snow, two
blue buttons, a red carrot, and a brown hat.

"Duggy Dog, you made the monster go
away!" cried Minty. "How brave of you!"

Jasper and Floss laughed.

"Any time, Minty," said Duggy Dog. "Now, how about coming to play in the snow?"

"How about some nuts? I don't like carroty noses," said the robin.

"There's a net of nuts hanging in the fir tree in my garden!" Minty called to the robin. "And of course I'll come and play, Duggy Dog."

"Thanks!" cheeped the robin, and off went Duggy Dog and his friends to play in the snow.